Treasury

Based on the NBC-TV Specials

Text by Dina Anastasio
Cover Illustrations by Phil Mendez
Text Illustrations by Roy Wilson

Scholastic Inc.
New York Toronto London Auckland Sydney

ISBN 0-590-40367-2

12 11 10 9 8 7 6 5 4 3 2 1   9   6 7 8 9/8 0 1/9

Printed in the U.SA.

TABLE OF CONTENTS

KISSYFUR AND HIS DAD

THE circus ringmaster walked to the center ring and raised his arms.

"Ladies and gentlemen," he shouted. "It is my pleasure to present Gus, the wonder bear, and his amazing cub, Kissyfur!"

Gus put his arm around Kissyfur and smiled.

"Are you ready, li'l bear?" he asked.

"Ready, Dad," Kissyfur said.

Kissyfur threw three balls into the air and rode down the ramp in front of Gus.

"Okay, son," Gus whispered. "Here we go."

Gus jumped on the teeterboard and sent Kissyfur flying through the air. Kissyfur flew higher and higher. Then he came to a stop on the high wire. The crowd cheered as Kissyfur balanced himself and took a bow.

That night, when Kissyfur and Gus were back in their cage, Gus pulled his son close to him.

"You know, li'l bear," Gus sighed. "I've been thinkin'. Maybe it's time to pull up stakes."

"You mean, leave the circus?" Kissyfur asked.

Gus nodded. "I'm tired of living in a cage," he said. "I want to be free. I think it's about time we found a new home. Don't you?"

Kissyfur thought that sounded like a wonderful idea. "When?" he asked.

"I don't know," Gus whispered. "But I'm working on it."

Kissyfur woke up very early the next morning. He leaned over and poked Gus.

"Hey, Dad," he said. "I think we're movin' on."

Kissyfur snuggled closer to Gus and watched as their cage was loaded onto the circus train.

When the clowns, horses, elephants, and acrobats were all on board, the ringmaster slammed the door. "Move 'em out!" he shouted.

The engineer sounded the whistle, and the train rolled off, leaving nothing but a muddy field behind.

The sky blackened as the circus train crossed a narrow bridge. Suddenly, a loud clap of thunder shook through the sky. Lightning struck one of the boxcars and sent it plunging into the water below. Water poured into the boxcar.

"Wh-what's happening?" Kissyfur cried.

"I dunno, li'l bear," Gus said. "But this might be our chance to escape."

Gus grabbed the cage door and shook it. He shook it harder and harder until the door broke loose from its hinges.

"Hang on, son," Gus shouted. "We're about to be free."

Gus raised his fist and poked a big hole in the top of the boxcar.

"Out we go," Gus said.

Side by side, they swam toward safety. By the time they reached land, the boxcar had sunk to the bottom of the river.

"Hey, Dad," Kissyfur whispered as he looked all around. "Are we free?" Kissyfur had never seen such tall mountains.

Gus and Kissyfur walked for a long time, searching for a new home. Toward dawn they came around a bend and stopped in front of a dark cave.

"Is this our new home?" Kissyfur said sleepily.

"I don't know," Gus told him. "Let's try it out."

Gus and Kissyfur found a smooth corner of the cave and huddled together.

"D-D-Dad," whispered Kissyfur. "I'm cold. I'm not sure I like this new home. Can we go back to the circus where it's warm?"

Gus shook his head. "Li'l bear," he said, "we have our freedom now. We'll find a better home. You'll see."

The next day, Gus and Kissyfur woke up bright and early to look for a new home. They walked and walked through the woods and into a swamp. After a while, Gus stopped and pointed to a big tree. "Look," he said. "This is it. It's perfect."

"Are we going to live in a tree?" Kissyfur asked.

Gus pulled Kissyfur closer to him and chuckled. "Just wait," he said. "You're going to love it."

The next morning, while Gus was working on their new home, Kissyfur went outside and sat on a log. He felt lonely and sad. He missed his friends at the circus.

"I want to go home," Kissyfur said out loud.

"Where's home?" a small voice answered.

Kissyfur looked up. "Who are you?" he asked.

"I'm Beehonie," a young rabbit answered. "And as I said before, where's home?"

When Kissyfur explained that he had lived in the circus, Beehonie looked puzzled. Beehonie had never heard of a circus before.

Kissyfur picked up three rocks and started to juggle them.

"Gee," Beehonie whispered. "That's swell."

Beehonie put her fingers between her teeth and whistled. In a few minutes, Kissyfur and Beehonie were surrounded.

"This is Duane," Beehonie said, pointing to a young pig.

"And that's Lenny," she said, pointing to a warthog.

"I'm Stuckey," said a sharp little porcupine.

"Toot is my name," said a little beaver.

Then Beehonie introduced her new friend and said, "Hey, Kissyfur. Show them your tricks."

Kissyfur did some tricks and everyone clapped.

"Since Kissyfur's new here," Beehonie said, "let's show him around."

Kissyfur spent the day exploring the swamp with his new friends. It was very late when he came back to the tree. Gus was waiting for him on the log.

"Close your eyes, li'l bear," he said. Kissyfur closed his eyes and took Gus's hand. Gus led him across the log and into the tree.

"Okay," Gus said. "You can open them now."

Kissyfur opened his eyes and smiled a great big happy smile.

"Your very own room, Kissyfur. Do you like it?"

Kissyfur didn't say anything for a few minutes. Then he hugged Gus around the knees and said, "It's the neatest room in the whole world."

"Welcome home, li'l bear," Gus said.

"Welcome home, Dad," said Kissyfur.

KISSYFUR AND THE NANNY

"ALL right, class," said Miss Emmy Lou. "Today we are going to do something very special. Mother's Day is coming up pretty soon, so we're going to make some Mother's Day cards."

"Oh, boy," shouted Lenny. "Mother's Day cards! That's great."

Kissyfur didn't think it was great at all. While his friends were cutting their papers into large heart shapes, Kissyfur slouched in his chair and watched them sadly.

Toot finished his card and showed it to Kissyfur.

"It's nice," Kissyfur said.

Toot looked down at Kissyfur's paper and crayons. "Where is your card?" he asked.

Kissyfur sighed and looked up at Toot. "I don't have a mom anymore," he whispered.

"Oh," Toot said. "I forgot."

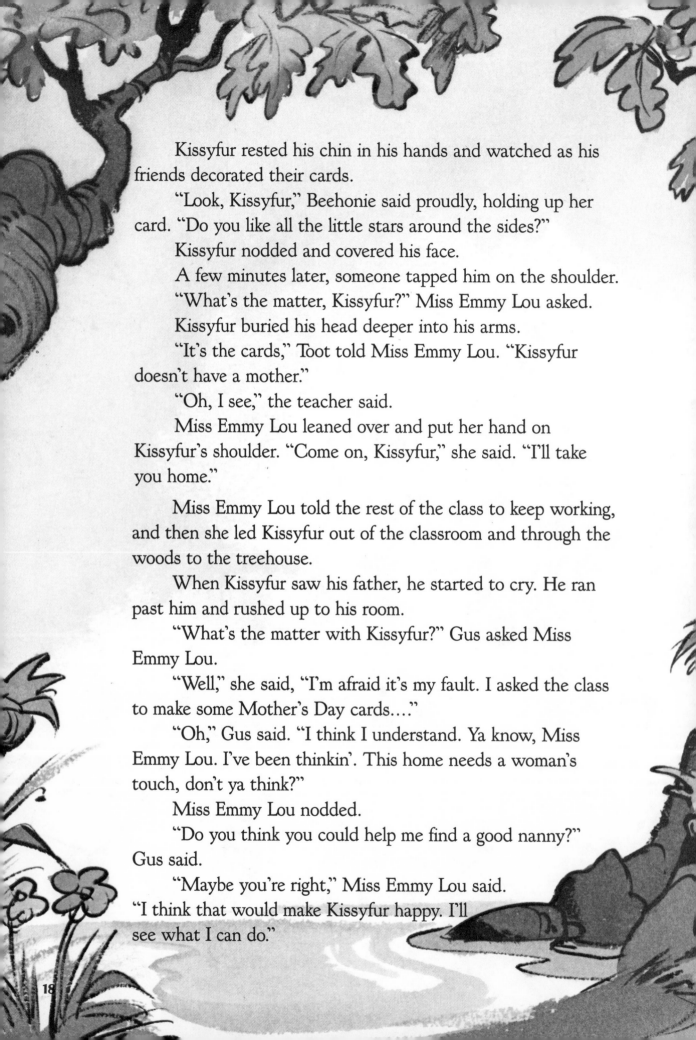

Kissyfur rested his chin in his hands and watched as his friends decorated their cards.

"Look, Kissyfur," Beehonie said proudly, holding up her card. "Do you like all the little stars around the sides?"

Kissyfur nodded and covered his face.

A few minutes later, someone tapped him on the shoulder.

"What's the matter, Kissyfur?" Miss Emmy Lou asked.

Kissyfur buried his head deeper into his arms.

"It's the cards," Toot told Miss Emmy Lou. "Kissyfur doesn't have a mother."

"Oh, I see," the teacher said.

Miss Emmy Lou leaned over and put her hand on Kissyfur's shoulder. "Come on, Kissyfur," she said. "I'll take you home."

Miss Emmy Lou told the rest of the class to keep working, and then she led Kissyfur out of the classroom and through the woods to the treehouse.

When Kissyfur saw his father, he started to cry. He ran past him and rushed up to his room.

"What's the matter with Kissyfur?" Gus asked Miss Emmy Lou.

"Well," she said, "I'm afraid it's my fault. I asked the class to make some Mother's Day cards...."

"Oh," Gus said. "I think I understand. Ya know, Miss Emmy Lou. I've been thinkin'. This home needs a woman's touch, don't ya think?"

Miss Emmy Lou nodded.

"Do you think you could help me find a good nanny?" Gus said.

"Maybe you're right," Miss Emmy Lou said. "I think that would make Kissyfur happy. I'll see what I can do."

Meanwhile, two hungry alligators were busy making plans.

"What's this?" Floyd asked as he rummaged through an old trunk he had found that morning.

Jolene walked over to the trunk and pulled out a purple dress, some high-heeled shoes, and a large head that looked like...

"A BEAR!" Floyd cried. "It's a BEAR!"

Jolene scratched her head and said, "I have an idea. Put on these duds and no one will know you're a gator. You can just walk right up to those snappy swamp critters and grab 'em for our supper!"

Floyd tried out his new disguise the very next morning. He tottered on high heels toward the paddlecab that would take him across the river and onto the main island.

As soon as he stepped onto Gus's paddlecab, Floyd felt two big arms around his shoulders.

"It's my new nanny!" Gus cried.

"Your new what?" Floyd asked, startled.

Gus hugged Floyd a little tighter.

"You're my new nanny," he said. "Come along, my friend, and I'll show you to your new home."

Gus took Floyd straight home without making another stop.

"Hey, Kissyfur!" Gus cried, as he opened the door. "Come and meet your new nanny."

Kissyfur ran into the living room and skidded to a stop.

"Well, Kissyfur," Gus said. "This is…"

Gus turned and looked at Floyd. "What did you say your name was?"

Floyd was shaking so hard that all he could say was, "M-m-m-me?"

Gus smiled. "Mimi," he said. "That's a nice name."

"Hi, Dad. Hi, Mimi," said Kissyfur. "I'll see you later. I'm already late for school."

At three o'clock, Miss Mimi was waiting outside the school.

"This is my new nanny," Kissyfur said to his friends. "This is Miss Mimi."

Miss Mimi leaned down and pinched Duane's rosy cheek.

"My, my, my, my," she said. "What a chubby one you are."

Miss Mimi pointed to Beehonie. "And who's this little lunch, er, little lady?"

"I'm Beehonie," the rabbit said.

Miss Mimi looked down at Beehonie and licked her chops. "Say," she said. "I have a splendid idea! How would all you little cubs like to go on a picnic?"

"A picnic!" cried Stuckey.

"Oh, boy!" shouted Lennie.

"Yayy!" laughed Toot. "It's picnic time."

The cubs followed Miss Mimi through the woods and into a small clearing.

"Here we are," Miss Mimi cried.

"At last!" shouted Toot. "I'm starving!"

"So am I!" said a raspy voice behind him.

The cubs turned. When they saw Jolene they scattered.

"GATORS!" shouted Duane and Kissyfur together.

Miss Mimi ran behind a tree and pulled out a cage. "Hurry," she cried. "In here. I'll handle this."

The cubs ran toward the cage, and when they were almost there, Miss Mimi pushed them inside and slammed the door.

"What's going on?" Kissyfur shouted.

Miss Mimi grabbed the sides of the bear head and yanked it off.

"It's Floyd!" cried the cubs.

"Oh boy!" said Lenny. "I knew this picnic was a dumb idea."

Kissyfur leaned over and grabbed the bars of the cage. "Wait a minute!" he whispered. "This is a wooden cage. Toot can chew us out of here."

While the gators were lighting the fire, Toot chewed. He chewed and chewed and chewed.

"Shhh," Kissyfur whispered. "Not so loud."

Toot gave the bar one more bite. "Yea!" shouted Lenny. "We're free!"

The cubs burst out of the cage and ran to safety.

That night, as Gus was turning out the light, Kissyfur handed him a card. "I made this for you, Dad," he said.

Gus took the card and looked at it. "It's a Mother's Day card."

"Yeah," Kissyfur whispered. "Cause you're the best dad... and the best mom...a cub could have."

WHAT'S COOL, KISSYFUR?

DONNA arrived at the swamp on the day that school let out. She was tall, pretty, and very, very cool.

"This is my niece, Donna," Miss Emmy Lou said. "She's going to stay with me this summer."

Donna pursed her lips and blew out the biggest bubble that any of the kids had ever seen.

"Gee!" sighed Kissyfur. "She sure is pretty."

"Where are you from, Donna?" Duane asked.

Donna put her hands on her hips and looked around. "Yellow-stone," she said, nonchalantly. "That's where all the best bears come from. There's lots to do in Yellowstone. What's to do around here?"

"Well," Toot said. "We go swimming, and we play swampball."

Donna shrugged her cool shoulders and let out a long, bored sigh.

"Swimming," she sighed. "How boring! Swimming's not cool."

Kissyfur looked at his friends and slicked back his hair. "What's cool?" he asked.

"I don't know!" Stuckey said. "Do you know, Duane?"

Duane shook his head and stared at Donna.

"Well!" she said. "I'll tell you what cool is. Cool is like me. It's doing whatever you feel like doing, and not letting anybody boss you around."

"Not even grown-ups?" Stuckey asked.

"Especially not grown-ups," Donna huffed.

"Hey," Lenny snorted. "I like it. How do we get to be cool?"

Donna walked around the kids and looked them up and down.

"I'd say that the first thing we do is start with your looks," she said. "Follow me, guys. When I'm finished with you, you'll be the coolest things goin'."

The kids followed Donna through the woods to Miss Emmy Lou's house. Donna led them up the stairs to her room.

"Okay, guys," she said as she took out a comb. "Let's get cool!"

When Donna was finished, she led them out of Miss Emmy Lou's house and back to the treehouse. Gus and Miss Emmy Lou were waiting for them.

"My," Gus said, "what do we have here?"

The kids glanced at Donna, and then they started to smile.

"We're COOL!" they shouted.

The grown-ups stared for a long time, trying to hide their smiles. Then Gus said, "Well, if you want to look like that, then fine. But right now, there's work to do, so let's go."

Gus started walking toward the other side of the swamp. As the kids followed, Donna grabbed Kissyfur's arm.

"Whoa!" she said. "I thought you weren't gonna let grown-ups tell you what to do!"

"This is different," Kissyfur said. "He's my dad."

Donna shrugged. "Whatever you want to do," she said. "But it's not cool."

Donna followed the kids through the swamp to a small creek.

"Wanna help?" Kissyfur asked, as they stopped beside a big log. "We're gonna make this log into the best bridge you've ever seen."

"Work is not cool!" Donna reminded them.

"Come on, Kissyfur," Gus shouted. "Grab that vine."

Gus had tied a large vine around one end of the log and was trying to pull it onto its end.

"Come *on*, Kissyfur!" Gus said again. "I need help!"

Kissyfur and the other kids ran over to the vine and started pulling on it. The log tilted up, up, up until it was resting on one end.

"Okay, now let it go," Gus said.

All at once, everyone let go of the vine. The log fell across the creek, forming a perfect bridge. They all cheered. All except Donna, who thought that the whole thing was too square for words.

"Okay, cubs," Gus said. "Start smoothing off the bark while I go find some railing poles!"

"Hey, you guys," Donna said, when Gus was gone. "Why don't you dudes ditch this crummy job and let's have some *fun!*"

Kissyfur scraped a small branch off the log and looked over at Donna. "We can't," he said. "My dad said —"

"Your dad?" Donna laughed. "Oh, brother, I thought you guys were cool!"

"I'm cool," Lenny snorted, jumping off the bridge.

"I'm cool, too!" Duane shouted, jumping off after him.

"How about you, Kissyfur?" Donna asked, smirking. "Are you cool?"

Kissyfur looked at Stuckey and Toot. Then he looked at Donna.

"Okay," he said. "I'm cool! I'm cool!"

"So, what cool things are we gonna do?" Kissyfur asked Donna as he followed her back toward the treehouse.

Donna pointed toward the paddlecab. "For starters, how about that?"

"My dad's paddlecab?" Kissyfur whispered.

Donna ran over to the paddlecab and jumped onto the bow. "Yeah!" she said. "Let's take this thing for a ride."

The kids followed Donna onto the paddlecab and sat down.

"Hey," Duane said, "where's Kissyfur?"

"I'm not supposed to," Kissyfur said.

Donna sat up and glared at him. "You're not chicken, are you, Kissyfur?" she said.

"Sissyfur's chicken! Sissyfur's chicken!" Lenny teased.

"Oh, yeah?" Kissyfur said, as he jumped onto the boat and sat down in the driver's seat. "Let's go!"

Kissyfur put his feet on the pedals and the paddlecab chugged out into the river.

"Now *this* is cool!" Donna shouted, and everyone cheered.

"That's nothing," Kissyfur cried. "Watch this!"

33

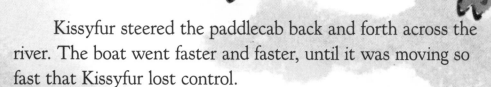

Kissyfur steered the paddlecab back and forth across the river. The boat went faster and faster, until it was moving so fast that Kissyfur lost control.

"Help!" Donna cried, from the bow of the boat. "Why don't you stop this thing?"

"Hit the brakes!" Lenny cried.

"There are no brakes!" Kissyfur reminded him.

"We're gonna crash!" Toot shouted as they sped toward the new bridge.

The shouts and cries reached the grown-ups, and they came running.

"Hold on, Kissyfur," Gus called. "I'm coming."

The big bear quickly dived into the water. Within moments, he boarded the paddlecab and took control of the wheel. Kissyfur looked up at Gus and smiled nervously.

"I think it was my fault, Dad," he said. "I wanted to be cool, so I took everybody for a ride."

Gus put his hands on his hips and frowned. "Cool, huh?"

"Yeah," Kissyfur whispered. "But you know what, Dad?"

"What, Kissyfur?"

Kissyfur dug his toe into the ground. "Well," he said. "I don't think I want to be cool anymore."

KISSYFUR IN THE MAGIC LAND

IT was a baking hot day in the swamp. Kissyfur and his friends sat in the shade of a giant tree.

"This stupid heat wave is drying up the whole swamp!" Lenny said. "We're running out of food and water—and the swimming hole is just a big puddle of mud."

"I wish there was something we could do," said Kissyfur.

"Looks like the heat's got you down," said an old buzzard from up in the tree.

The kids nodded.

"Well," said the buzzard. "I know a place where the swimming hole is filled with cool water, and the grass is green and soft, and there is plenty to eat."

"Plenty to eat?" Kissyfur whispered. "Where is this place?"

"Just follow me up this magic tree," said the buzzard. "And by the way, the name is Flo."

The cubs quickly climbed up the tree. One by one, they made their way through the clouds.

The magic land was on the other side of a river. Kissyfur saw the top of the cliff and the garden filled with trees and flowers and fountains.

"It's even better than Ms. Flo said," Duane whispered, coming up behind him.

"It's incredible!" Stuckey said.

"Let's check it out!" Kissyfur cried as he led the others across a small bridge and into the magic land.

But while the kids were exploring the magic land, two mean, hungry alligators were searching for food below.

"Well, well," one of the gators said. "I do believe that those are cub tracks. And I bet they're hiding up in that tree!"

"I'm so happy I could scream!" Stuckey shouted, as he peeled his fourth banana.

"I'm so glad you like it," said a voice in a tree above him. "Are you all enjoying yourselves?"

"Oh, yes, Ms. Flo," shouted the kids.

"Good, good!" said Flo. "Now eat hearty. Put a little meat on your bones."

Stuckey picked up a pile of fruit that he had stacked beside him and started to gobble it up. All of a sudden he heard a strange hissing sound behind him. "What's that?" he whispered.

Flo chuckled. "Oh, don't mind him," she said. "That's just Reginald. Say hello to our friends, Reginald."

The head of a huge snake appeared over Flo's wing and peered down at the kids.

"Oooh, yesss!" hissed Reginald. "I just looove meaty bones."

The kids stared up at Reginald. Reginald stared back at the kids.

"Oh, don't mind him," chuckled Flo. "He just means he loves little swamp cubs."

Kissyfur was beginning to get nervous. "I think we should go," he said. "We'll see you tomorrow."

"Nonsenssssssssse," Reginald hissed as he curled his big pointy tail around Kissyfur's ankle.

Kissyfur picked up his other foot and stomped it down on Reginald's tail. As Reginald was nursing his sore tail, Kissyfur and his friends dashed off.

"Run!" he shouted. "They're after us!"

Reginald and Flo chased the kids past the pool, around the fruit trees, and right up to the river.

"Hurry!" Kissyfur cried.

Duane grabbed Kissyfur by the arm and pulled him back. "Wait!" he said. "Look!"

"GATORS!" cried the kids.

Kissyfur looked behind him. Reginald and Flo were gaining fast. And the gators were almost upon them.

"This river has to go somewhere," Kissyfur said. "Jump on that log!"

The kids piled onto a large log that was floating by. "Hang on!" Stuckey cried. "This is gonna be one fast ride."

The log bounced down the river, whirled through a cavern, soared over a waterfall, and landed right under the bridge.

"Over the bridge—and fast!" shouted Kissyfur.

As the kids followed Kissyfur to the top of the magic tree, they heard the hissing sound once again.

"It's Reginald," Beehonie said. "Hurry!"

Kissyfur turned around. The gators were close behind, followed by Reginald and Flo.

"Faster, faster," Kissyfur cried.

As the cubs quickly shimmied down the tree, Beehonie had an idea.

"Chop down the tree!" she shouted.

As soon as the cubs reached the ground, Toot used his sharp teeth to cut down the tree.

"Safe at last," said Lenny.

The swamp cubs looked around and saw the familiar sights of Paddlecab County.

"This is better than magic," Beehonie said.

"Yeah," Kissyfur laughed. "It sure is good to be back home."